BIBAS SUSITRENKĖ GALVĄ

BIB BUMPS ITS HEAD

Ronald Leunissen

ISBN: 9798550969694

Imprint: Independently published

Translation: Margarita Leunissen

Original titel: Bib bumps its head

# BIBAS SUSITRENKĖ GALVĄ

# BIB BUMPS ITS HEAD

## Ronald Leunissen

Tai yra Bibas.
Bibas yra žirafa.
Bibas mėgsta bėgioti.

This is Bib.
Bib is a giraffe.
Bib loves to run.

Žiūrėkite į tai!
Bibas bėga.
Bibas begioja labai greitai.

Watch this!
Bib is running.
Bib is running very fast.

Tai yra šaka.
Šaka pagaminta iš medžio.
Šaka kaba žemai.

This is a branch.
The branch is made of wood.
The branch is hanging low.

Bibas nekreipia dėmesio.
Bibo galva atsitrenkia į šaką.
Ai!

Bib is not paying attention.
Bib's head hits the branch.
Ouchie!

Tai yra Bibas.
Ant galvos yra didelis guzas.
Gumbas skauda.

Here's Bib.
There's a big bump on its head.
The bump hurts.

Tai yra gydytojas.
Bibas yra pas gydytoją.
Gydytojas uždeda pleistrą.

This is the doctor.
Bib is with the doctor.
The doctor places a band-aid.

Pleistras yra ant galvos.
Pleistras padengia guzelį.
Bibas nebejaučia skausmo.

The band-aid is on the head.
The band-aid covers the bump.
Bib doesn't feel pain anymore.

Bibas vėl bėga.
Bibas linksminasi.
Bibas vėl greitai bėga.

Bib is running again.
Bib is having fun.
Bib is running fast again.

Vėl yra šaka.
Bibas bėga link šakos.
Ar tai baigsis gerai?

There's the branch again.
Bib is running towards the branch.
Will this end well?

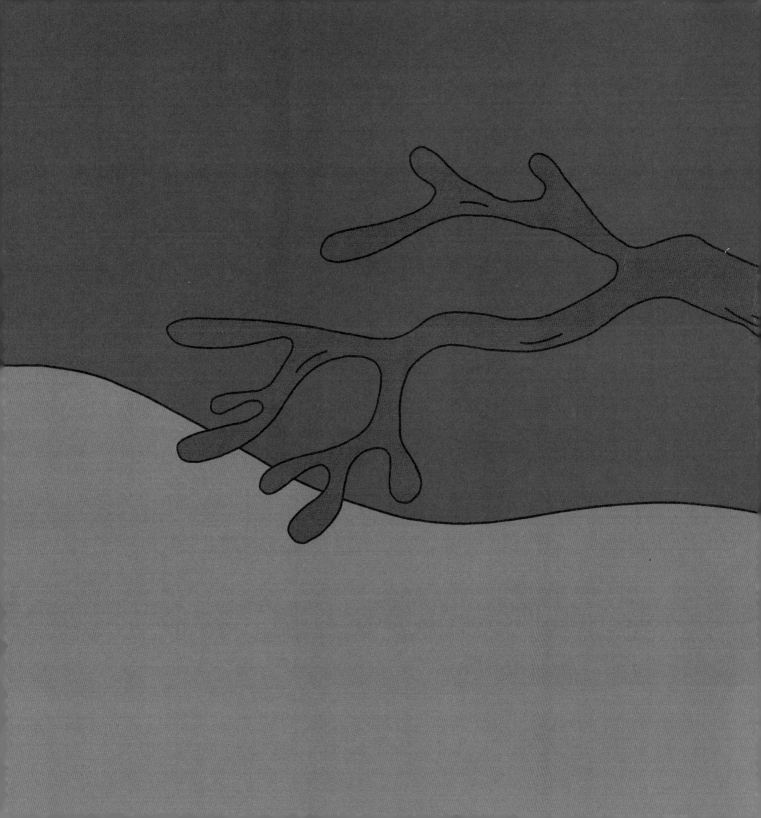

Taip! Sekasi gerai.
Bibas laiku nuleidžia galvą.
Bibas praeina pro šakele.

Yes! It goes well.
Bib lowers its head in time.
Bib passes under the branch.

Štai akmuo.
Akmuo yra žolėje.
Bibas nemato akmens.

There's a rock.
The rock is in the grass.
Bib doesn't see the rock.

Oi! Nesiseka.
Bibas akmenį pamato per vėlai.
Bibas skrenda oru.


Oh! This is not going well.
Bib sees the rock too late.
Bib flies through the air.

Štai Bibas.
Vėl ant galvos yra guzas.
Gumbas skauda.

Here's Bib.
There's a bump on its head again.
The bump hurts.

Labas, Bibai, sako gydytojas.
Tu ir vėl čia?
Gydytojas uždeda kitą pleistrą.


Hi Bib, says the doctor.
Here again?
The doctor places another band-aid.

Tai yra Bibas.
Bibas dabar turi du pleistrus.
Abudu ant galvos.




There's Bib.
Bib now has two band-aids.
Both on its head.

Bibas vėl bėgs.
Bet pirmiausia Bibas atsisveikina.
Iki pasimatymo! Iki kito karto!


Bib is about to run again.
But first Bib waves goodbye.
Bye Bib! Until next time!

Printed in Great Britain
by Amazon